CURIOSITY SHOP

CURIOSITY SHOP

PICTURE PUZZLES TO SEARCH AND SOLVE

A CanYou See What I See? BOOK

WALTER WICK

CARTWHEEL BOOKS

AN IMPRINT OF SCHOLASTIC INC.

NEW YORK

First published in Japan in 2021 by Shogakukan Asia Pte. Ltd. under the title *Can You See What I See?: Curiosity Shop.*

Library of Congress Cataloging-in-Publication Data available

ISBN 978-1-339-01669-6

10 9 8 7 6 5 4 3 2 1   24 25 26 27 28
Printed in China   38
This edition first printing, August 2024

The text type was set in Asap. The display type was set in Copperplate.
Book design by Walter Wick and Charles Kreloff

TO LINDA

TABLE OF CONTENTS

ENTRANCE

*Can you see
what I see?*

A gumball machine,
a fork, a spoon,
a tower of bricks,
a sun and moon;

a watering can,
a whistle, 2 bells,
a bowler, 3 boats,
and 7 seashells;

a curious cat,
a red lobster plate —
now step inside,
more treasures await!

THE MARIONETTES

*Can you see
what I see?*

A caterpillar puppet,
a long wooden nose,
a welcoming jester
with bells on his toes;

7 elephants,
a teapot for tea,
2 drummers drumming,
4 ships at sea;

3 striped animals,
2 rabbits, a fox,
and a hand mirror hidden
in a jewel-filled box!

BINS & BOXES

*Can you see
what I see?*

A mouse, 10 cats,
2 hands of cards,
a pig, 2 penguins,
3 royal guards;

a lamb, a lobster,
a berry that's red,
5 dragonflies,
a needle to thread;

a peacock, a panda,
a key, 2 locks —
now let's peek inside
that button box!

BUTTON BOX

*Can you see
what I see?*

A downhill racer,
a tennis ace,
a jolly old king,
a bulldog face;

3 folding fans,
a dragon's long tongue,
6 swans, 2 trumpets,
a spring that's sprung;

a fork, 3 bridges,
an old TV,
and a hand that's pointing
to number 3!

THE PEARL CHEST

*Can you see
what I see?*

A bee, 4 bunnies,
4 owls, too,
a monkey looking
right back at you;

2 doves, a dancer,
a blue fish tail,
a phone, 3 footprints,
a frog, a snail;

a unicorn horn,
a lone silver wing,
2 starfish,
and an eyeball ring!

UNDER THE STAIRS

*Can you see
what I see?*

3 pyramids,
a bridge that's red,
a waving cat,
a spool of thread;

a cave, 3 castles,
a ring of keys,
2 Ferris wheels,
a pair of skis;

2 full moons,
a broken clock's spring,
4 dinosaurs,
and a girl on a swing!

FLIGHTS OF FANCY

*Can you see
what I see?*

A flying castle,
a leaf-shaped kite,
a daring rescue
on a moonlit night;

4 telescopes,
a horse and wagon,
3 anchors, a pencil,
a flying dragon;

2 airmail deliveries,
a fish on a chain,
3 boats with sails,
and a man in a train!

WIND-UP TOYS

**Can you see
what I see?**

A trick dog's coin,
a songbird's house,
3 violins,
a car-driving mouse;

2 tambourines,
a harmonica, too,
a watering can,
a baby kangaroo;

a well-dressed fish,
red and black checks,
2 juggling clowns,
and a bear cleaning specs!

ODDS AND ENDS

**Can you see
what I see?**

3 safety pins,
2 electric guitars,
an ON/OFF switch,
a bus, 8 cars;

a calculator,
a bug, a bike,
a lion key,
3 frogs, a trike;

a cowboy boot,
a covered wagon,
a crown, an ax,
a skull, a dragon!

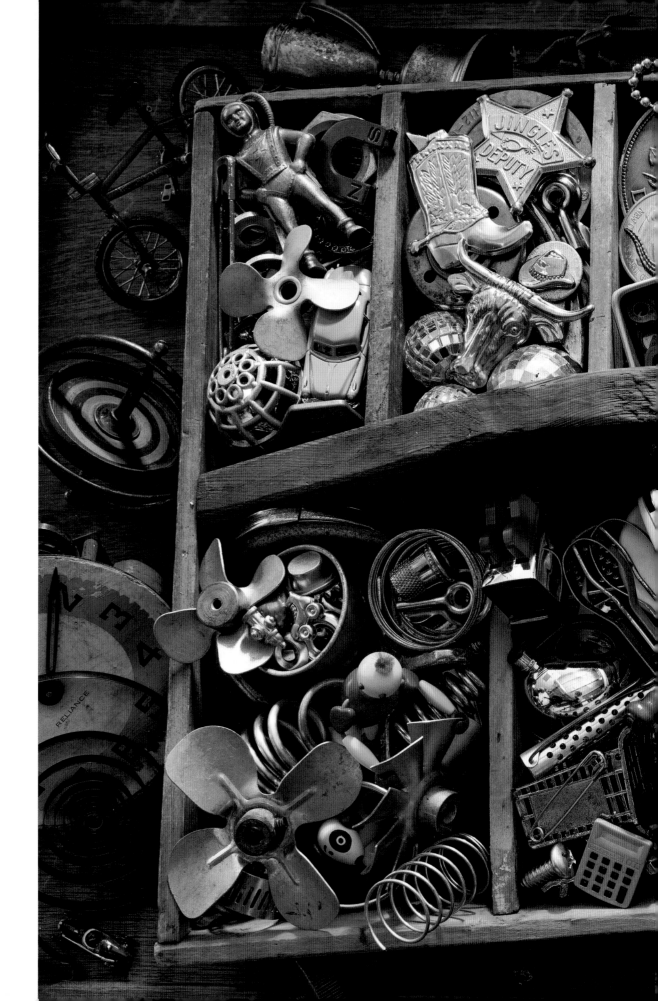

GLASS IN THE WINDOW

*Can you see
what I see?*

6 butterflies,
9 birds, a frog,
a blue giraffe,
a musical dog;

a shark, a lobster,
a flower ring,
a fish in a beak,
a knot in a string;

a cat's curly tail,
a glass dinosaur —
now head upstairs,
there's more to explore!

UPSTAIRS

*Can you see
what I see?*

A silver airship,
an astronaut,
3 lighthouses,
a pretty teapot;

4 umbrellas,
2 spoons, a spider,
5 giraffes, 6 dogs,
a horseback rider;

a planet that's blue,
a rooster that's red,
and gold eyeglasses
on the shop ahead!

CLOSING TIME

Can you see
what I see?

3 clock faces,
3 trucks, 6 trains,
a zebra, 3 pigs,
4 hammers, 2 planes;

an ice-cream cone,
a racket, 3 dice,
4 rabbits, 2 squirrels,
2 curious mice;

a pair of skis,
and an old wooden top —
that's all, my friends,
time to close up shop!

ABOUT THIS BOOK

The idea for this book began with a simple thought: What if I gathered together my sizable collection of props — vintage toys, out-of-fashion buttons and baubles, mismatched miniatures, and other oddball items — put them on display under one roof, and invited everyone to come for a tour. What would I call such a place? The answer came easily: a *Curiosity Shop*. The realization of this idea was another matter. If at first I thought artfully photographed arrangements of my collections would do, I soon imagined a two-story building packed to the rafters, curated by a shopkeep with a special interest in unusual forms of air travel. With the scope of the project thus expanded, my collections grew, too — by way of online searches and frequent repeat visits to thrift stores and antique malls.

One year later, I've fulfilled my promise. With this book, I invite readers on a tour of my shop — a *Curiosity Shop*. In the end, the shop itself is the curiosity. Could the mountains of items scattered among these pages really be contained within that miniature building? The jester that greets us just inside the entrance wants us to believe this is so. True, he is a jester, after all, but in a spirit most important to my readers, in the realm of imagination, anything is possible.

ACKNOWLEDGMENTS

I'd like to thank Heather Aylsworth, who assisted with the photography, set-building, and props, including making the jester's costume; Randy Gilman, for his beautifully crafted curiosity shop model and airship; and Linda Cheverton Wick, whose artistic wisdom and guidance have been a driving force behind my books for 30 years. I'd also like to thank my editor, Kyoko Kiire, of Shogakukan Inc., Japan, for fully supporting this project even after the start of a global pandemic that put everything in doubt; Shigesato Itoi for his translations from English to Japanese; and my agent, Maiko Fujinaga, at Japan Uni, for her guidance. For this U.S. edition, I'm grateful to Scholastic Inc. for their continued support, especially Ellie Berger, Executive V.P. and President of Trade Publishing; Publisher-at-Large, Ken Geist; and Associate Editor, Jonah Newman.

Walter Wick

ABOUT THE AUTHOR

Walter Wick is the photo-illustrator and writer of the internationally bestselling Can You See What I See? series as well as the photo-illustrator of the globally acclaimed I Spy series, with riddles by Jean Marzollo. He is also the author and illustrator of the award-winning *A Drop of Water: A Book of Science and Wonder*, and its recent follow-up, *A Ray of Light*. His photo-puzzles have appeared in *Games* magazine and in the *New York Times*, and a retrospective of his work featuring large-scale photographs has been exhibited widely in museums in the United States and in galleries in Japan. He lives with his wife, Linda, in Miami, Florida.

More information about Walter Wick is available at walterwick.com.